D1452009

PERFECTLY POPPY

The Story of Poppy, the Cross Beak Chicken

Always be You !!!

Written by **Tricia Stone-Shumaker**

Illustrated by **Kim Sponaugle**

Perfectly Poppy
The Story of Poppy, The Cross Beak Chicken

Written by Tricia Stone-Shumaker
Illustrated by Kim Sponaugle

Copyright 2021 by Tricia Stone-Shumaker

All rights reserved. No part of this publication may be reproduced, distributed, or transmitted in any form or by any means, including photocopying, recording, or other electronic or mechanical methods, without the prior written permission of the publisher, except in the case of brief quotations embodied in critical reviews and certain other non-commercial uses permitted by copyright law. For permission requests, write to the publisher, addressed "Attention: Permissions Coordinator," at the address below.

PO Box 403
Lemoore, CA 93245

FIRST EDITION

ISBN: Softcover   978-1-7365289-0-7
         EBook   978-1-7365289-2-1

PERFECTLY POPPY

The Story of Poppy,
the Cross Beak Chicken

For my husband Scott and sons, Forrest, Skye and Zak.
My heart and support.

Gratitude to Kelli Anderson, fellow Chicken Mom
Extraordinaire. Poppy is thriving, thanks to your
knowledge and experience.

For all those with special needs and their families.
This book is for YOU.

Poppy, the friendly little chicken,
has a beak that points two different ways.

Poppy groans, "Oh, I feel so alone."

Remi, the neighborhood duck,
hears Poppy's weeping tone.

"Chin up, my friend, I say it's true! Being different makes you . . . YOU. You see, I cannot walk on my own. I have one foot and one foot alone. But that doesn't stop me from wanting to roam."

Remi has a plan and
is hoping Poppy is a fan.

"Poppy, come on a trip with me, oh would you please? We can explore everything from the seas to the trees. I will show you that even far from home, you are really not alone."

So, Poppy and Remi begin on their drive.
And they are so excited, they dance a little jive.

They visit the blue ocean where Poppy meets a school of fish. But the fish blubbers, "Look at that chicken. He is different. His beak is tweaked!"

That makes Poppy sad while the fish shriek, "Eeek!"

Trish the fish, who is missing a fin and can't swim, says, "I'm different too. But that's okay. Change your point of view. The things that make you different are the things that make you . . . YOU."

So, Poppy and Remi continue on their way.
And to all the fish, Poppy says, "Good day."

Next, they visit the hot desert where Poppy meets a swarm of snakes. But the snakes sneer, "Look at that chicken. He is different. His beak is tweaked!"

That makes Poppy sad while the snakes shriek, "Eeek!"

Scotty the snake, who can't slither, says, "I'm different too. But that's okay. Change your point of view. The things that make you different are the things that make you . . . YOU."

So, Poppy and Remi continue on their way.
And to all the snakes, Poppy says, "Good day."

Next, they visit the flowery hills where Poppy meets a band of horses. They neigh, "Look at that chicken. He is different. His beak is tweaked!"

That makes Poppy sad while the horses shriek, "Eeek!"

Howie the horse, whose voice is hoarse, struggles to say,
"I'm different too. But that's okay. Change your point of view.
The things that make you different are the things
that make you . . . YOU."

So, Poppy and Remi continue on their way. And to all the horses, Poppy says, "Good day."

At last, they visit the grassy fields where Poppy meets a flock of chickens. They bawk, "Look at that chicken. He is different. His beak is tweaked!"

That makes Poppy sad while the chickens shriek, "Eeek!"

Charlie the chicken, whose beak points two different
ways, says, "I am different too. The other chickens make
fun of me. Boo hoo! But I am just like you."

Poppy tells Charlie, "Chin up, my new friend. Change your point of view. The things that make you different are the things that make you . . . YOU."

Poppy smiles from ear to ear
and bawks, "I can now see that being
different makes me . . . Me."

> "There is no greater disability
> in society than the inability
> to see a person as more..."
> -Robert M. Hense

The Author
Tricia Stone-Shumaker

Tricia Stone-Shumaker is a speech language pathologist and author who was raised in California's Central Valley. She runs her own private practice where she specializes in autism, myofunctional disorders and early intervention treatment.

Tricia lives on a hobby farm with her husband Scott, that is filled with a variety of animals. But it was an incredible journey with a few of her critters that has changed her outlook on life.

In 2020, she and Scott travelled 11,000 miles across the US in an RV with two dogs, a duck and a chicken. The trip earned them a spotlight in local and national media and inspired her to write about their adventures, focusing on her special needs chicken, Poppy.

An advocate for inclusion for all, she believes we should not allow a disability to get in the way of our dreams.

In the future, Tricia intends to write more about Poppy's adventures and has a series of three books planned, with speech therapy materials included in each one.

You can contact or follow Tricia Stone-Shumaker at:

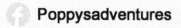 Poppysadventures   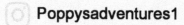 Poppysadventures1   tricia@poppythechicken.com

www.poppythechicken.com | www.stonespeech.com

CPSIA information can be obtained
at www.ICGtesting.com
Printed in the USA
JSHW050722170521
14841JS00002B/3